ANIMAL BABIES

BABY PORCUPINES

by Jennifer Boothroyd

Consultant: Beth Gambro
Reading Specialist, Yorkville, Illinois

BEARPORT
PUBLISHING

Minneapolis, Minnesota

Teaching Tips

Before Reading

- Look at the cover of the book. Discuss the picture and the title.

- Ask readers to brainstorm a list of what they already know about porcupines. What can they expect to see in this book?

- Go on a picture walk, looking through the pictures to discuss vocabulary and make predictions about the text.

During Reading

- Read for purpose. Encourage readers to think about porcupines and the animal life cycle as they are reading.

- If readers encounter an unknown word, ask them to look at the sounds in the word. Then, ask them to look at the rest of the page. Are there any clues to help them understand?

After Reading

- Encourage readers to pick a buddy and reread the book together.

- Ask readers to name three things porcupines do between the time they are born and the time they are ready to have babies. Go back and find the pages that tell about these things.

- Ask readers to write a sentence and draw a picture of something that they learned about porcupines.

Credits:

Cover and title page, © puttle712/Shutterstock; 3, © Farinoza/Dreamstime; 5, © Dssimages/Dreamstime; 6, © Rosa Jay/Shutterstock; 7, © Don Johnston_MA/Alamy Stock Photo; 9, © Panther Media GmbH/Alamy Stock Photo; 10, © Michael Quinton/Minden Pictures; 11, © kajornyot/Getty Images; 12, © Mysikrysa/Dreamstime; 15, © Warren Metcalf/Shutterstock; 16, © Pascale Gueret/iStock; 18-19, © Mizu001/iStock; 21, © Don Mammoser/Alamy Stock Photo; 22, © critterbiz/Shutterstock; 23BL, © bucky_za/iStock; 23BM, © jeep2499/Shutterstock; 23BR, © Anankkml/Dreamstime; 23TL, © Awei/Shutterstock; 23TR, © Holly Kuchera/Dreamstime

Library of Congress Cataloging-in-Publication Data

Names: Boothroyd, Jennifer, 1972– author.
Title: Baby porcupines / Jennifer Boothroyd ; consultant, Beth Gambro.
Description: Bearcub books edition. | Minneapolis, Minnesota : Bearport
   Publishing Company, [2021] | Series: Animal babies | Includes
   bibliographical references and index.
Identifiers: LCCN 2020030866 (print) | LCCN 2020030867 (ebook) | ISBN
   9781647474713 (library binding) | ISBN 9781647474799 (paperback) | ISBN
   9781647474874 (ebook)
Subjects: LCSH: Porcupines—Infancy—Juvenile literature.
Classification: LCC QL737.R652 B66 2021 (print) | LCC QL737 .R652 (ebook)
   | DDC 599.35/971392—dc23
LC record available at https://lccn.loc.gov/2020030866
LC ebook record available at https://lccn.loc.gov/2020030867

For more information, write to Bearport Publishing, 5357 Penn Avenue South, Minneapolis, MN 55419.

Printed in the United States of America.

Contents

It's a Baby Porcupine!

Watch out!

A mother porcupine has sharp **quills**.

But her **newborn** is soft.

The baby opens its eyes.

The little porcupine **wiggles** its body.

It is about as big as a jug of milk.

This cute baby is called a **porcupette**.

Say *porcupette* as POR-kyuh-pet.

The porcupette crawls to its mother.

It drinks milk from her body.

Slurp!

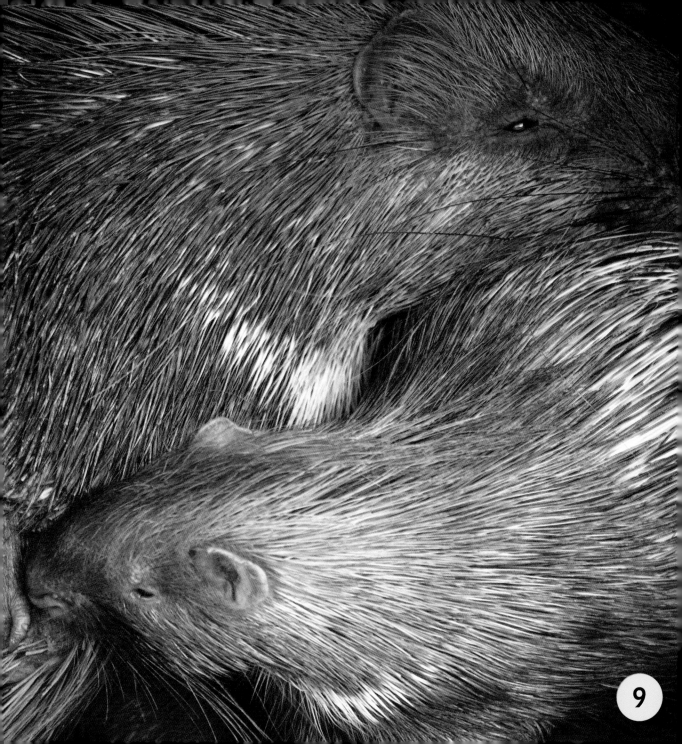

The baby's quills start to get hard in a few hours.

They will **protect** the porcupine.

Quills keep it safe.

The sun comes up.

It is time to sleep.

Zzzz!

When the sun goes down,
it will be time to wake up.

In a couple of days, the baby starts to eat plants.

Munch, munch, munch.

It uses its large front teeth to bite.

The porcupine gets bigger and stronger.

Sharp claws help some porcupines learn to climb.

They help some learn to dig in the ground.

After a few months, the porcupine leaves its mother.

It is ready to live on its own.

A porcupine is fully grown in two years.

Soon after, it can have babies of its own.

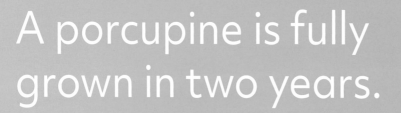

The Baby's Body

Quill

Tail

Eye

Claw

22

Glossary

newborn just born

porcupette a baby porcupine

protect to keep something safe

quills sharp spines outside an animal's body

wiggles moves something back and forth

Index

milk 8

mother 4, 8, 18

plants 14

quills 4, 10, 22

sleep 13

teeth 14

Read More

Leaf, Christina. *Hedgehog or Porcupine? (Blastoff! Readers: Spotting Differences).* Minneapolis: Bellwether, 2021.

Sherman, Jill. *Porcupines (North American Animals).* Mankato, MN: Amicus, 2019.

Learn More Online

1. Go to **www.factsurfer.com**
2. Enter "**Baby Porcupines**" into the search box.
3. Click on the cover of this book to see a list of websites.

About the Author

Jennifer Boothroyd enjoys visiting museums and nature centers.